Blue's Sniffly Day

by Brigid Egan
illustrated by Victoria Miller

SCHOLASTIC INC.

New York Toronto London Auckland Sydney
Mexico City New Delhi Hong Kong Buenos Aires

For Jessica Lissy—B. E.
To Lissa, Mommy loves you—V. M.

Note to Parents from Creators:
In *Blue's Sniffly Day*, Blue's friends confront a real-life problem—Blue has a cold and isn't feeling well enough to play with them. While exploring concepts of empathy and friendship, this book gives children a chance to build their visual perception skills. We hope reading *Blue's Sniffly Day* will spark discussion with your child about how friends can care for and support one another.

Based on the TV series *Blue's Clues*®, created by Traci Paige Johnson, Todd Kessler, and Angela C. Santomero as seen on Nick Jr.®
On *Blue's Clues*, Steve is played by Steven Burns.

No part of this publication may be reproduced in whole or in part, or stored in a retrieval system, or transmitted in any form or by any means, electronic, mechanical, photocopying, recording, or otherwise, without written permission of the publisher. For information regarding permission, write to Simon Spotlight, an imprint of Simon & Schuster Children's Publishing Division, 1230 Avenue of the Americas, New York, NY 10020.

ISBN 0-439-39887-8

12 11 10 9 8 7 6 5 4 3 2 1   2 3 4 5 6 7/0

Printed in the U.S.A.

First Scholastic printing, March 2002

Hi! Have you seen Blue? She's been under the weather for a few days, and we want to find out how she's feeling.

We thought you might want to play, Blue. But it doesn't look like your sniffles have gone away yet.

What can we do to make Blue feel better?

Look, Blue! Dr. Shovel and Nurse Pail are making a house call.

Can you spot anything in the room that Shovel and Pail might need for their pretend doctor's visit?

Hmm . . . it looks like Dr. Shovel and Nurse Pail's pretend checkup isn't going to help cure Blue's real cold.

Maybe Mailbox has something to make Blue feel better.

Mail's here! Blue's friends from school sent her a get-well card!
Get Well Soon, BLUE! We Miss You!

What a nice card! It really helped to
cheer Blue up.

Blue is going to take a nap now. But after all that sneezing, she wants to wash her hands first.

Good idea, Blue! I'll help you.

Can you tell which towels belong to Blue?

You know, when I don't feel well, I like to hold Horace, my anteater. Horace always makes me feel better.

Let's see if we can find a stuffed animal for Blue to hold. Do you see any?

Maybe reading a story will help Blue feel better. Is that a good idea, Blue? Blue?

Blue's asleep! Well, maybe sleeping will make her feel better.

We can all try to be very, very quiet so Blue can sleep.
How quiet can you be?

This quiet?

Even quieter.

You're so good at being quiet! Why don't we tiptoe down to the kitchen and see what Mr. Salt, Mrs. Pepper, and Paprika are up to? Come on.

Allo, Steve! We're making homemade soup . . .
. . . to help Blue get over her sniffles!

Will you help us find the rest of the ingredients from Mr. Salt's recipe? You will? Great!

We want to give Blue the biggest bowl of soup. Can you find the biggest bowl?

Let's pour some orange juice for Blue. Can you find an orange cup for her juice? What else should we put on her tray?

I think sleeping made Blue feel a little better. Now she's ready to enjoy the soup we made. Thanks for helping Blue to feel better!